Wrangler Jayne
&
Gypsy Rose

By Master Coe

MC Publications

ISBN-13: 978-1-60965-021-6

ISBN-10: 1-60965-021-2

Table of Contents

Chapter One

Alone in the night

I hate these fucking bastards. I lived here my entire life. My father hasn't been in his grave for two days and they are auctioning off our land as if we were vagabonds. The bank called our note due. No one there will even speak with me about extending credit.

Even if I sold off what little steer we had left, it still wouldn't come close to what we owe. Some asshole bought our prime stock the first day. He didn't even have the nerve to show his fucking face. He used a proxy and paid cash. So, here we are.

If they think they are going to get my Daisy, they're going to have to pry my dead body off this mount. She's my prize pinto. We won the barrel run two years standing. We're a team.

"Jayne." A gentle familiar voice breaks her concentration. "You don't have to be here."

"Yes, I do Jake." She stares ahead, avoiding his gaze purposely. "I want them to see me."

He brings his horse next to hers. "They know who you are. They just felt this would be better than a bunch of strangers, buying up the property."

"Strangers leave. I'll have to look at these people every day for the rest of my life."

"You'll survive."

"As what? The butcher's wife?"

"Would that be so bad? Clayton is a hard-working young man. One day he will inherit his father's market."

"I'm a rancher, not a housemaid."

"You're a pain in my ass. That's what you are. We fixed up a spare room for you."

"I aren't taking no charity. Not even from you Jake."

"Where did you learn to speak English young lady?" Before she could respond, "This isn't charity. I can use a good ranch hand." Jake reaches out and place his hand on her shoulder. "Anything you need out of the house?"

"No. Anything of value or that means a shit, I loaded up in that old covered wagon. I hid it behind the willow trees out back."

"I'll have one of the hands go fetch it and bring it to my barn. You can sort through it tomorrow."

>Fighting back tears, for the first time Jayne glances over at him. A faint whisper passes through her thin lips, "thank you."

>He reaches into his satchel and hands her a couple of sandwiches and a cantina of water. "Sarah and the girls said you wouldn't come back right away. So, they made these to keep you from starving." He tips his hat and turns to ride off. "Dinner is at five. We're having some sort of dumplings. Sarah said if you're late, you do the dishes alone"

>They share a brief smile as he rides off.

I guess I was hungrier than I thought. I finished both those sandwiches in nothing flat. Sarah does make the best corn beef sandwiches in these parts. I just wish I had some of her slaw to go along with it.

I must have lost track of time perched under that old shade tree. When I next looked up the sun was hanging low in the sky and the auction was breaking up for the day. It's Saturday, so bright and early next Saturday the fucking scavengers will return to pick over the carcass.

I gathered myself and walked Daisy off quietly into the woods. When I was out of sight, I doubled back to where I stashed that old wagon.

I almost panicked when I didn't see it in the distance. Then I recalled, Jake said he would send a hand to fetch it. I mounted Daisy and headed on to Jake's ranch.

I must have dozed off in the saddle. Good thing Daisy knew the way. I was sent down there at least twice a week for one thing or another. I was awakened by the sweet savory aroma of fresh baked bread and Sarah's chicken dumpling. I picked up the pace to a slow trot and headed for the barn to bed down Daisy in one of the stables.

I was stopped by Riccardo, just outside the barn doors. "Are you trying to get trampled on Ricky?"

"You get along inside. I'll tend to Daisy."

"I'll tend to my own mount, thank you kindly."

"When the boss lady says to me, when Jayne arrives have her wash and get ready for supper. That's what I do."

"The boss lady?" I couldn't help but laugh. His fancy accent was a hoot.

"If I have to toss you over my shoulder and dunk you in the trough myself, I will."

I looked over at the filthy drinking trough and gave him my best sneer? "You and what army?"

In nothing flat he tossed me over his massive shoulders. I couldn't help but run my hands down his muscular back.

Just as he was about to toss me in, I gave in gripping firmly to his belt. "Okay, okay! I can wash myself. If you don't mind?"

He gave my bottom a firm smack. It sorts of caught me off guard. I wasn't expecting that. It stung but didn't really hurt. "I have a mind to dunk you anyways."

Leave it to me to get all girl like, "Ricky please." I purred in a soft voice. Where in the fuck did that come from?

He let me down gently and gave me two more sharp smacks across my bottom. "Now get."

I actually giggled and twisted my hair, looking back at him as my weak knees struggled to keep my balance as I fluttered off. Somebody shoot me.

Grant it, he's quite good looking for an old guy. He has to be at least 28 or 30. At the age of 20, most of the old hags around here consider me to be an old maid. I have much better things to do then push out a herd of loud ass children for some fat ass drunk. I just don't know what that is yet.

Ricky sat directly across from me at dinner. I swear he was staring right through me the entire time. I just couldn't ever catch him. After Dinner Ricky and Jake went off to the study to smoke cigars, while his sons finished their chores. I helped Sarah and their daughters, Katherine and Catalina clean up in the kitchen. I called them Kit and Cat, or Kit-Cat if I wanted them both. They were twins so it seems to fit.

I admit I was a bit jealous of Ricky. Not because he got to smoke. I hate cigars. I knew they were discussing the upcoming cattle drive. I could manage a herd as good as any man. I miss being out with my dad for weeks as we delivered our herd to the slaughter house.

In a house full of people, I never felt so alone in my life. When we turned in for the night, I had a room all to myself and I felt crowded. I had to get some air and clear my head.

I hadn't planned on being out long. I stepped into some slippers and through on an old robe Sarah lent me until I could unpack. I stepped out back and sat on the rear porch for a spell. I must have over slept. I woke up to a roster crowing in my ear.

I figured I was already out here, so I might as well go rustle up some eggs. I hate chickens. For one they are mean. Also, they are messy. They just drop their egg anywhere. You have to take care not to step on an egg, or something worse. The girls did good. I filled my basket and there were plenty left over for market. I closed up the coop and headed back, like a good little dairymaid.

I placed the eggs in the pantry and headed back to my room to clean up and dress for breakfast and pick out an outfit for church. I wasn't all that excited about church. But, afterwards was the annual fair. So, I had to pick out and outfit for that as well. I signed up for the barrel run but wasn't quite sure I would compete this year.

After breakfast and our chores were done, I hitched Daisy to the back of the wagon. Kit-Cat and I loaded ourselves into the back of the wagon. Kit-Cat started speaking that gibberish, only they understood.

Ricky trotted alongside us as if he owned the road. I paid him no never mind. I found a crawl space under some piles of hay. There was plenty of loose straw on the boards to make a decent cushion. It kept the sun off me and I was able to catch some shuteye on long boring trip.

Once we arrived it took us about 20 minutes to pick the straw from our hair and clothes. I don't know what was worse, the hypocrites staring at me with false pity or Pastor Wilkens shameless sermon on tithing. Heaven forbid the church is cheated out of its fucking share of the win fall.

Wrangler Jayne & Gypsy Rose

Afterwards I passed through the gauntlet of false sympathy and 'If you ever need anything, we're just down the road a piece.' I wanted to tell them all to fuck off and go to hell. But then I would have to do a counselling session with Sister May. I hate that bitch. Besides I had to get out of this dress.

I found the stable in the barn where Daisy was and changed there. I figured I'd hide out there for a spell and avoid the cooking chores. I much rather help put the final touches on the fair itself. I know it's boys work, but at least I don't have to pluck any chickens.

As Jayne stood up after putting on her boots, she almost fell over in shock. She found herself staring face to face with Riccardo, as he peered over the stall door.

"How long you been standing there?" Jayne barked with a shaken voice.

"Long enough. Gal you must be the fastest dresser I've ever seen. I didn't get to see much." A sinister sneer came over his face. "Not that there's much to see."

"Oh, there's plenty to see!" She prompted up her almost nonexistence breast. "They just aren't for your eyes. Now get!"

He slowly entered the stall and latched it behind him. She had time to walk out past him but, she knew he wouldn't force himself on her.

He backed her into a corner. He slid his worm rough hands up under her shirt and cupped her entire left soft tender breast.

"What are you doing?" She whimpered.

"Gal if you have to ask, I'm doing it wrong."

"We shouldn't be doing this. What if someone walks in?"

He reaches under with his free hand and cups her other breast. "There will be nothing to see. If you want to finish this, you're going to have to meet me at the old shed after the race."

"Who said I was going to race?"

"Oh, you'll race."

"What if I lose and not in the mood for your nonsense?"

He squeezed both her nipples as hard as he could. "You'll win. You don't know how to lose."

The pain quickly turned into an excitement she's never felt before, nor ever imagined. He slowly released his grip and slid his hands down her back and from under her shirt. It was all she could do to stand as her legs quivered beneath her.

"After you win, meet me in the woodshed."

All she could do was nod in compliance.

He quickly turned and walked away as if nothing had happened.

Jayne fixed her cloths and readied Daisy for the race.

Daisy knew we had a race to win as I lead her out from the barn. She trotted along as if they had already hung that winner's reef around her neck. The race isn't until midafternoon, but she needs the fresh air.

I warm her up by taking her on short walks to get the blood flowing through her legs. Some like to do practice runs. But that just fatigue the mount. I may walk her through the course once or twice, but nothing more than that.

I didn't eat much. I never do before a race. But I did make sure I had some of Sarah's slaw and sweet potato pie.

Daisy was flawless in the barrel run. I was a bit worried in the third turn. Daisy leaned in more aggressively than usual. I was sure she would slip or clip the barrel. My first instinct was to try to slow her down. I fought that urge, because I knew it would end bad for the both of us.

I guess she knew what she was doing. She shaved three seconds off last year time. It was almost not enough, but Jimmy fought his horse in the final turn causing him to lose traction. They didn't fall, but it caused them to come in a second behind us. I was glad we won, but I was even happier, Jimmy and his mount weren't hurt.

After leading Daisy back to the barn from the winner's circle, if you could call it that. I saw Riccardo start to make his was over towards the old woodshed. I took my time at the stable and tended to Daisy.

After tending to Daisy, I spent about an hour or so at the fair, before making my way to the shed. I didn't want to seem too eager or just disappear and have people wonder where I was. I told Sarah I wanted sometime alone, and I would make my way back with Daisy before bedtime. Sarah had a thing about girls being home at a certain time.

Riccardo was visibly agitated at having to be made to wait for so long. He wasn't accustomed to waiting, especially for a woman.

When Jayne came face to face with Riccardo, she leaned in slowly to kiss him. At the last moment she turned away, "I don't think this is a good idea". A baleful half smile came over her face as her back was turned to him.

He took her by her arm and spun her around and held her securely in place. "What the hell are you playing at gal?"

"I'm not playing at anything." She looked up and pressed her body closer to his. "You're just not my type."

He cupped her ass and lifted her up onto her toes. "I'm everyone's type." He backed into the shed forcing her onto her toes and off balance.

He backed her onto the back wall. She wrapped her legs and arms around him, to regain her balance. "Has anyone ever told you, that you have a big head?"

Before Jayne could make her next nervous wise crack, Riccardo had her pants and panties down around her ankles. If it weren't for her boots they would have fallen to the ground. He wasted no time in stepping out of his pants and underwear.

He pressed her backwards. She held onto the cross beams on the wall for support. He grabbed her pants and lifted her knees to her chest.

Riccardo had no trouble entering Jayne. She was wetter than he expected. He wasn't gentle, but Jayne didn't need gentle. She needed a release. Jayne gave as good as he gave. With every thrust into her she grinded him deeper inside of her. Soon, she was fucking him more than he was fucking her.

The sensations searing through Jayne's body was greater than anything she could have imagined. She managed to free her left leg. She leaned her weight forward, forcing Riccardo to the ground onto his back. Jayne rode his shaft up and down as deep as she could take.

Jayne had what she thought were orgasms before when she masturbated. This was different. Her entire body was electrified and pulsed. She had never felt anything like it before. She could feel her juices rush through her as the inside of her vagina pulsed and gripped his cock.

She could feel him about to explode. He pulled out and released his massive load across her sweat covered ass and up her back.

"What the fuck?", Jayne exclaimed. "Why did you do that?"

"Unless you want to become pregnant, I can't cum inside of you."

Jayne rolled off him and onto her back. "Fuck me."

Riccardo looked over at her with a Chester cat grin on his face. "I just did."

Without looking at him, Jayne raised her right hand and gave him the middle finger. "Don't flatter yourself Ricky."

He sat up and patted Jayne's still extended and extremely sensitive clitoris. Jayne's entire body pulsed bringing her close to another orgasm.

Riccardo stood up and pulled up his pants. "You should get dressed, before someone come looking for you."

Jayne just glared at Riccardo as he left. She couldn't control the pulsation rushing through her body. It took a bit, but she composed herself enough to get dressed.

Fuck that was intense. I didn't expect to lose control like that. My legs are still a little shaky. I was planning on riding Daisy home. I think I will ride inside the wagon. I feel energized and extremely relaxed.

What really piss me off is I feel like his bitch. I'm actually fantasizing about the next time. What the fuck? I'm not going to become anyone's fuck toy. I'm definitely not going to marry him or any other man. But damn, he was good.

The blood sucking leaches didn't bother me as I walked around the fair. The only thing that bothered me, was the way I kept looking over my shoulder, hoping to find Ricky. I'm glad I didn't see him for the rest of the fair.

The ride back didn't feel as long as the ride there. Even Kit-Cat's gibberish didn't bother me.

When we arrived, I tended to Daisy. Then I turned in for the evening. We completed our chores before we left, so there wasn't anything for us to do.

Chapter 2

The Last Roundup

I couldn't help but go back home to view the carnage. Those fucking vultures picked the place clean in only two weekends. They even took the fucking candle holders. Of course, some unknown buyer purchased our house and land. Fuck, I don't even have a home anymore. How fucked up is that?

I should burn this fucking place to the ground. My father built every inch of it with his own two hands. How can I destroy that? No matter who lives here, this will always be my home. One day I will buy it back.

Fuck this sentimental bullshit. What's done is done. The way back was slow and quiet. Daisy was in no rush. She kept her head low for the most part.

I had planned to take a nap when I got back. As I rode up, I noticed Jake and his crew about to ride out with the heard. What the fuck? That's my father's brand. That asshole Jake bought my father's prime stock.

> Jayne storms over to Jake. "What the fuck, Jake? Where have you been hiding them? I hope you stole them at a good fucking price."
>
> Jack gave Jayne a sharp slap across her face. Not hard, but enough to get her attention. "First young lady, you know better than to speak to me like that. I didn't steal anything. Your father gave them to me for safe keeping, about a year ago. I moved them to the far side of the ranch, just before the auction." He reaches out and take Jayne by her hands. "When we return, I will give you the money I receive for your father's cattle."

Jayne pulls her hands away. "I'm coming with you. I've been driving my father's cattle since I was six."

Jake shakes his head in defeat. "You are your father's daughter. We leave after lunch."

"I'll load my wagon and hitch the rig."

"Riccardo wanted to bring additional ammo and supplies. I guess we can use your wagon for that. Get with Riccardo before we head out." Jake walks over to Riccardo.

Those bastards were going to leave me. They think I'm weak. Especially Ricky. He's been trying to turn me into some sort of paper doll since the fair. He actually bought a fucking ribbon for my hair. What the fuck, was that all about?

After lunch I finished packing my wagon and tied down the cover. I hitched two of Jake's horses to my wagon. They have made this drive before and they should be used to the terrain. I left Daisy behind. She's a fine mount, but I don't want anything to happen to her.

Jayne notices Riccardo walking away from the front of her rig. She walked over to see what he had done. She was not expecting what she found. "Ricky! What the fuck is this?"

Riccardo stops and turns to face Jayne. "It's a dog. You have seen one before?"

"I know what it is! What is it doing on my wagon?"

With a smile Riccardo answered, "It's your dog."

Jayne is clearly agitated. "What?"

Riccardo walks over and starts petting the dog. "He's a German Shepard. The breed isn't really adapted for cattle drives. But they ware great for keeping coyotes, wolves and other predators away. They make excellent watch dogs. They can sniff out an intruder before we can see them."

"I don't care what type of dog it is. What the fuck is it doing on my wagon?"

"I thought I told you, he's your dog."

Jayne's face is now bright red. "I don't want a dog. I don't need a dog. Get rid of it."

Riccardo walks over and starts adjusting Jayne's hat. He knows how much she hates for anyone to touch her hat. "If you're going to ride with us. That is not only your dog, he's your responsibility. Otherwise, you can just stay home."

Jayne pushes Riccardo away. She's contemplating shooting him in his leg. "Whatever. What's its name?"

"It is a he and he doesn't have a name yet. You will have to name him."

Jayne looks over at the dog and walks over towards it. "He looks like some sort of fucking bear. I'm going to call him Bear and teach him to bite you."

Riccardo kisses Jayne on her check and walks away. "You do that sugar pants."

Jayne looks at the dog and point's to Riccardo. "Get him Bear. Bite him. Just the leg." Bear wags his tail and licks Jayne's face. Jayne sighs and gives Bear a hearty rub on his neck and behind his ears. "We have a lot to work on."

The ride to auction was uneventful. Jake had trade agreements with most of the tribes. The others we avoided. It took about a week to make the drive. We had to stop and let the heard feed, water and rest.

For the most part Bear rode on the wagon with me. He walked along side of the wagon every now and then. At night he slept in the wagon with me. If anyone approached my wagon while I slept, he would wake me with a low growl. If he detected a predator, he would slip out under the rig's cover and chase it off. Afterwards he would sleep on the buck boards for the remaindered of the night. Okay, he's growing on me. I'm not fucking heartless.

I've never been to an auction before. It reminded me of the vultures picking over my father's ranch. Dad sold directly to a few slaughter houses. We would get our money, usually in the form of a note, upfront.

The banker was onsite and wired the notes to Jake's account. For a fee of course. Jake cashed out what he needed for supplies for the trip back.

Early the next morning we returned, Jake took me into town to collect the pay for the crew from the bank. I took my father's long riffle, just in case.

After he got the cash to pay the crew, Jake took me over to the same banker that refused to extend our loan. We sat down at his desk.

Jayne glares at the banker. "Why are we here?"

Jake replied, "I'm opening you an account."

She looks over at Jake and stands up to leave. "Not at this bank you're not."

Jake takes Jayne by her hand. "Sit down. What happened before was business. You had no collateral and your father had extended past his maximum credit. The bank had no choice but to foreclose."

Jayne looked at Jake, while fighting back tears. "That wasn't just business. That was personal. My father put his life into that ranch. Find another bank."

Jake wiped away the tears Jayne couldn't contain. "This is the largest bank in the territory. They are protected by the Pinkertons."

"Fine. What do you need me for?"

"You need to sign some paperwork, to make everything legal. It will also allow you to add money and notes to your account and take money out as needed. You can also wire notes between banks."

"So, I could take it all out and keep it in a safe, back at the ranch?"

"You could, but this bank pays the highest usury. You would miss out on as much as 1 to 2% a year. Also, as soon as word got out, every bandit within 200 miles will come looking for you and your money,"

"So, the bank will pay me to keep my money in the bank?"

Jake places his hand on Jayne's shoulder. "How much you get depends on how much the bank makes from the use of your money with investments and loans. Understand?"

"Not really, but I trust you." After Jake looked over each form, Jayne signed and initialed as instructed. She stopped when Jake placed one of the forms in front of her. "What's this?"

"You need to sign next to the X. That's the deed to your ranch."

"I don't own a ranch. It was auctioned off."

"I bought the house and the land. It was enough to cover the debt your father left. Your father was a good businessman. He made a bad investment. Many people lost their homes and land behind it. Now I'm giving it back to you. It belongs in your family."

Jayne began to tear up again as she looked up at Jake. "You mean I have a home?"

"You've always had a home. You will always have a home. But yes, you have your home back."

It took Jayne a few seconds to steady her hand, before she could sign the paperwork for the deed. The banker handed Jayne the deed to her father's ranch. In a low voice Jayne responded, "Thank you."

I couldn't control myself. After the banker handed me the deed. I turned around, grabbed hold of Jake and buried my face deep into his chest. I cried uncontrollably like a fucking baby. I so much wanted to say thank you, but that word somehow seemed so small. I had no words to describe the overwhelming joy and relief I felt. All I could do was cry.

Jake made me leave the deed at the bank in a safe deposit box. I didn't want to let it go. But he was right. I had no safe place to keep it at home.

On the ride home, I kept reaching over and hugging Jake. I almost caused us to run off the trail a few times.

When we returned to the ranch, I stayed on the wagon while Ricky took it into the barn to unhitch the horses and break down the wagon.

Once we were far enough into the barn, I motioned for Ricky to follow me to the back of the covered wagon. I intended to tell him about my trip into town. When he climbed into the wagon, it didn't go quite as planned.

I knocked him over onto his back. I pinned him to the floor and planted a deep kiss across his unsuspecting lips.

Ricky wasted no time in flipping us over, removing my boots and pants. I was so wet; he slides inside of me with no resistance. Every inch of my body was

Wrangler Jayne & Gypsy Rose

on edge. He thrusted so hard and deep I could feel every time his balls slapped across my ass.

The harder Ricky fucked me, the more I thrusted back in response. It became a competition. Until it became so over whelming to me, I couldn't breathe.

I finally surrendered. I gripped his shoulders, wrapped my legs around him as tight as possible. I allowed him to have his way with me. The deeper I dug my nails into his back, the harder he fucked me.

I could feel myself cum several times. It was uncontrollable. But, why would I want to control something as exhilarating as that.

This time, he pulled out and cum across my stomach. I must have fallen asleep. The next thing I remember is Ricky slapping me across my bare ass.

"Get dressed. I need to break down the cover," Riccardo stated. He tossed Jayne a wet towel and a dry one.

Jayne started to clean up and get dressed. "Oh yeah, guess what?"

"What?"

"I have my father's ranch back. Jake bought it from auction and gave it to me."

"I'm happy for you. Your father was a good man." He taps Jayne's leg. "Hurry up, before Jake comes looking for us."

At dinner Cody, Jake's five-year-old son, sat in my lap most of the time. Cody loved to cuddle. Jacob, Jakes' oldest son at twelve, ignored me as usual. He hadn't discovered girls yet. Give him another year, before he loses his mind. He already has the girls chasing him.

After dinner, Jake invited me into the study. He didn't offer me a cigar, but this is where he discussed business. I was so excited, I wanted to burst.

Jake leaned forward towards Jayne. "I know how stubborn and self-sufficient you are. I held back from auction a dozen heifers and two bulls. That's not enough to go into business right away, but it is a start to a solid herd."

Jayne was at a lost for words. She uttered softly, "Thank you. I don't know what else to say. If we had all of this, why did we lose the farm?"

"The banker found out your father was sick. He refused to extend your father an additional loan." Jake leaned back into his chair. "Your father and I came up with a way to pay off the mortgage and leave something behind for you. It took us a few years, but we got it done. Too bad he wasn't here to pass this down to you himself."

"Riccardo and the other hands will be off for a few weeks. They need time off. When they return, I will send Riccardo to fetch the heard."

"It'll give me time to clean the place up."

Chapter 3

Clayton's Proposition

I couldn't sleep the entire night. All I could do
was think about how beautiful that od ranch was. To
think, I almost burnet it down. I was up early that
morning. I got a head start on my chores. I was so
excited. I even completed some o Kit-Kat's chores.
After breakfast, Daisy, Bear and I were off to take
a look at our home.

Jake insisted that I stay with Sarah and him at
least until Riccardo and the others returned and
had time to fetch the heard. Of course, he was
right, I couldn't stay there alone. It would take
some time to hire a trust worthy crew.

As I rode up, I noticed another horse, hitched to
the post. The horse looked familiar, but I couldn't
match it to a face.

Bear's head dropped low and his tail stuck straight
out. The hair on the ridge of his back stood right
up. He had a deep growl. I've never seen him like
this before. Tt was sort of scary at first, but I
felt protected.

I didn't know where to look for the intruder first.
Bear knew exactly where to look. He went to the
door of the old smokehouse. The door was closed, or
Bear would have gone right in. He crotched down
low. His ears were back. His growl became a roar,
as he crotched his body to the ground. Despite his
stance, Bear looked twice his normal size. Bear was
no more than nine months old. I don't know how
effective he could be. He sure in the hell is
scaring the fuck out of me.

> Jayne dismounted Daisy and took cover behind a
> water barrel. "I don't know who the fuck you
> are. You had better come out with your hands up
> or I'll start shooting."

The door slowly opened a crack and a voice came out. "Take it easy. I'm coming out." As the door slowly opened, Bear tried his best to force his way in. The man inside fought to keep the door closed, but Bear kept prying it open. It was all the man could do to hold the door closed enough to keep Bear out. "It's me!" the voice called out.

"Who in the fuck is me?" Jayne replied.

"Clayton!"

"Who?"

"Clay!"

"The butcher's son?"

"Yes!"

"What the fuck are you doing here?"

"Would you call off your fucking wolf?" Clayton's voice was full of stress. He was fighting a losing battle to keep Bear out.

Jayne let out a sharp loud whistle. "Bear! Come here." To her surprise he came over to her side. He kept a close watch on the smoke house door. Jayne returned her pistol to its holster. She wrapped her arms firmly around Bear. "Alright, but don't make any sudden moves. I don't know if I can hold him."

"What do you mean you don't know if you can hold him? Why do you have a bear if you can't control it?"

Jayne rolled her eyes. "He's not a bear, he's a dog."

"I heard you call him a bear."

"Trust me, he's a dog. His name is Bear."

Clayton slowly poked his head out. "Where is it?"

"Clay, if you don't get your ass out here, I'm going to pull you out by your fucking ears."

Clayton slowly emerged from the smoke house. He kept the door open, in case Bear decided to attack.

Jayne looked at and pointed towards Bear. "Stay here." Bear laid down, keeping Clayton in his sights. Jayne walked over to Clayton. "You're such a pussy."

Clayton snips back. "Who walks around with a fucking bear?"

Jayne motions for Bear to come to her.

Clayton's voice went up a pitch. "Don't call that mother fucker over here!"

"How else is he going to get to know you? Just don't piss your panties."

Bear immediately started sniffing Clayton.

"Girl, if this thing eats me, I'm going to haunt you."

"He's just getting to know who you are."

Soon Bears posture turned more relaxed. He started wagging his tail. He even gave Clayton a few licks on his hand.

Clayton slowly started petting bear. "I swear girl, you're going to be the death of me."

"I'm not the one, sneaking around other people's property. What the fuck do you want?"

"I wasn't sneaking. I just wanted to see what kind of condition this old thing was in. I have a business proposition for you."

"Let's go inside. They took everything. I think my old bed is still there. At least we will not have to sit on the floor."

Clayton followed Jayne inside the house. He kept a close eye on Bear. Bear didn't enter the house. Jayne tied Daisy o the hitch next to Clayton's horse. He laid down at the front door. They made their way back to Jayne's old room and sat on the corner of her bed.

Jayne was curious. "What is this business deal?"

"It's more of a proposition."

"Excuse me?" Jayne ask with a puzzled look on her face.

Clayton blushes, "Not like that. I'm tired of being known as only the butcher's son. I want to open my own smokehouse."

"Wouldn't it be easier to open a smokehouse in town? Your father has a shed you can convert into a smokehouse."

"I could do that but, I would still be the butcher's son. I saved almost every cent I've earned working for my father. It's not a lot, but it is enough to fix up an existing smokehouse."

"What does that have to do with me?"

"I went to the bank to find out who bought the ranch. They told me it was signed over to you. I came to take a look and make sure I could fix it up, before I approached you."

Jayne replies with sarcasm. "So, you figured I would just drop my pants, spread my legs and give you my smokehouse, because you're a good fuck?"

Clayton leans slightly into Jayne. "I wasn't going to lead with that. I was suggesting a fifty-fifty partnership. After expenses of course."

"What makes you think I would go for this? Or if it will even work?"

"I know my craft and my customers. The nearest smokehouse is over 70 miles away."

"I don't know." Jayne knew she didn't know anything about running a smokehouse.

Clayton leaned in and kissed Jayne firmly on her lips. "Then plan B it is."

Jayne pulls back slightly. "What makes you think you're that good?" Normally she would have pushed Clay away. It has been a while since the fair. Riccardo seemed to have been avoiding her. She was quite horny.

Clayton knew he would never get a chance like this again. He leaned in and kissed Jayne passionately. The first thing he did was remover her holster.

"Coward." Jayne whispered between breaths.

They frantically started undressing each other. Clayton pushes Jayne back onto her bed. Jayne wraps her legs around him as she laid flat on her back with him on top of her. She could feel his cock on the verge of penetrating her. She takes a deep breath and slowly sighs as his cock slide slowly inside of her.

His cock was thicker and longer than she imagined. She held on tight as he slowly moved his shaft in and out of her.

Jayne whispers in his ear, "Faster."

Clayton increases his speed. He was only moving his cock half ways in and out, never putting it all the way inside of her.

"Deeper", Jayne whispered. She could feel him fill her completely with each thrust. "Harder.

I won't break." She dug her nails deep into his back.

Clayton pulled Jayne's head back by her hair. She wasn't expecting that. He let out a loud deep gasp and loosened her grip on his. Her legs went limp and she gripped her bed with both hands. It was all she could do to hold on as he pounded away at her.

Just after Jayne's second orgasm her entire body went limp. Clayton was on the verge of exploding. He pulled out and did the unexpected. She prepared herself for an explosion of his hot cum across her stomach.

He tightened his grip of her hair. Moved up to her face and slid his cock deep into her unsuspecting mouth. She gagged as he cock slid partially down her throat. She struggled at first. She had never had a man's cock inside her mouth. Once she caught his rhythm, she began to enjoy it. Then something else unexpected occurred.

His hot cum exploded down her throat. She gagged and flailed her legs wildly as she choked while swallowing half of his load in one gulp. He cum so much it dripped from the sides of her mouth and nose. He held her head in place until he expelled his complete load. Her reflexes forced her to swallow what she couldn't expel with his thick cock stretching her mouth open to its limits.

When he unstartled her she jumped out of bed and ran out side butt naked. She went over to the water pump and started pumping it frantically. As the water began to flow, she washed her face and the remaining cum from her mouth. Clayton admired the perfection of her body as he observed her washing his cum out of her hair, from the safety of the bedroom window.

When Jayne returned to the bedroom, Clayton was stretched out across the top of the bed, still completely nude. She climbed into bed next to him and struck him several times with open palms.

"Fucking asshole. What was that all about?" Jayne barked.

Clayton pulled her close to him. "You never had a man cum inside your mouth before?"

"No, that was disgusting." Jayne looked up at him. "You could have at least warned me." She gave him one more sharp smack and then rested her head onto his shoulders.

Jayne was awoken by the roster crowing. She couldn't believe they had slept the entire night.

She nudged Clayton. "Wake up Clay. It's time we get going." She jumped out from bed and started getting dressed.

"What time is it?" Clayton asked.

"It's morning. Sarah is going to kill me."

"Just tell her you fell asleep in your old bed." A Sinister smile fell across Clayton's face. "In away that's true. So, you won't be lying to her."

Jayne rolled her eyes and shook her head. "Get dressed so we can go."

"So, what about my proposition?"

"I'll let Jake and Sarah know you will be coming by for supper. Afterwards we can go over it with Jake. If he feels it's a good idea, I'm all in."

She didn't start back until after breakfast. She had to wash and dry her bed sheets before she left.

She was getting hungry and she knew Bear was starving. She pulled off the trail, shot, prepared and cooked two rabbit. She got in the habit of keeping old bowl with her when she traveled with Bear. She poured some of the water from her cantina into it for him. She watered down Daisy before they headed out.

Bear ate all of his rabbit and begged at least half of her rabbit as well. She broke down the site and headed back to Jake's.

I got back in time to complete my morning and mid-day chores. Jake wasn't there when I arrived. Sarah said he went into town and would return by supper. Sarah said it was okay for Clayton to eat with us tonight.

Sarah didn't ask where I met up with Clay. No one said anything about where I was. They did give me looks that made me uneasy. So, I let it go.

When Jake finally arrived, he looked upset. I was going to ask if everything was alright. Kit-Kat stopped me and said I should let it go for now and give him room. Okay, I don't know what the fuck that meant. I took their advice. I figured it had to do with business.

Dinner went well, I guess. Kit-Kat were usually quiet. They usually speak their twin gibberish nonstop. After Dinner Jake listened to what Clay had to say.

To my surprise Clay was very businesslike. I don't usually get excited over men talking business. But Clay was impressive. He answered every question Jake threw at him. Jake agreed to Clay's proposition. He had one condition. Jake had to oversee the smokehouse as well as the ranch for at least a year. Of course, Clay and I agreed.

Jake had me wait in the study as he walked Clay out. I felt like I was missing out on something. I didn't want to jinx the deal, so I waited.

When Jake returned, he sat on the edge of his desk. Before Jayne could say a word, Jake asked "Do you know the rule about when you girls are to return home?"

Jayne's voice became shaky. She felt like a child. "Before sunset." She cleared her throat and continued. "I'm sorry. I fell asleep on my old bed and lost track of time."

"With Clayton there, as well?"

Jayne could feel her heart in her throat. "He was there when I arrived. That's when he told me about the smokehouse. I didn't understand the details, so it took a while to explain it to me. I feel a sleep on my bed. He was on the floor. Nothing happened."

"That's fine, this time. In the future get home before sunset. If you plan to stay overnight at the farm, let us know. Otherwise you have to be more responsible." Jake stood up and started to walk away.

These next words should have never come out of my mouth. I was home free. But me being me, I had to get the last dig in.

In her snottiest tone Jayne replied. "It's not as if I could have sent a carrier pigeon."

Jake became enraged. He took Jayne by her arm forcing her onto her toes. He led her out of the study and out of the house.

Crap, I should have just said yes sir. I could have just apologized but, that would have been too simple as well. I'm such a dumb fucking cunt sometimes.

I dug in and tried to resist when I saw we were headed towards the toolshed. He flung me over his shoulder like a sake of potatoes. I started crying before we made it to the shed. By the time we entered I was balling like a little bitch. How humiliating.

Before he let me down, he unfastened my pants and yanked my pants and panties down to my ankles. He sat on a stool, pulled me across his lap. He wrapped his right leg around the back of my legs, locking them into place. He pushed my head down forward. My face was inches from the ground and my bare ass was fully exposed.

I don't know where he got that fucking hair brush from. He lit my ass up with it. He had me locked so securely I couldn't get my hands behind to protect my ass. I couldn't even wiggle.

I was wet before the first stroke fell. After the first few minutes I was dripping. At least it felt like a few minutes.

> With each stroke Jake stated firmly. "You will never speak to me like that again. Do you understand?"

I had to struggle to catch my breath as I answered. With every stroke I screamed yes sir! I was so hoping that fucking hairbrush would just break. He showed no mercy. I haven't been spanked since I was a child. I have never been spanked this hard in my life.

When he finally let me up, I fell to the ground. I just knew my ass was bleeding. I reached back to rub it. I could feel the heat. I couldn't stand to touch my own ass. One good thing is that there was no blood. He never broke my skin.

Wrangler Jayne & Gypsy Rose

Jake left me crying and flailing on the ground, without saying a word. Besides my ass being on fire I was dripping wet. He never said a word about it. I know he had to have noticed. You can't miss something like that.

When I was finally able to pull myself together, I looked for a clean rag. I wet it and wiped down my pussy and legs. My clit was so sensitive, my body convulsed every time I rubbed or brushed lightly over it. How fucking embarrassing.

Chapter 4

Lost but not alone

It took a few days for me to be able to sit on my ass. L let Jake and Sarah know that I was going to drop off a few things at the house and I may stay over the night. Sarah made me a couple sandwiches to hold me over.

Jake wanted me to wait until tomorrow morning. Riccardo and the crew were returning later today. I convinced him that I would be alright. He told me he would send Riccardo and a few of the boys around in the morning, after breakfast.

I took a few of the things I was able to save from those fucking vipers. It wasn't a heavy load. I was able to hitch just one horse to the wagon. I used Thunder. Cody named him. I left Daisy behind. I don't like hitching her to rigs. Bear jumped up onto the wagon as I pulled out.

As I pulled up to the ranch, I half expected to find Clay in the smokehouse. But he wasn't. I don't know why, but I was disappointed. Oh well, it was most likely for the best. The last thing I need is for Ricky to walk in on us. Not that it's any of his business. But you know.

I pulled the wagon into the barn. I unhitched Thunder and started off loading. I didn't move anything into the house right away. I had to figure out where I wanted to put everything. Not that I had a lot.

Ricky was bringing the heavy stuff like the dining room table and chests. I would have to go into town later and buy proper furniture. Sarah and Kit-Kat are going to help with that.

I shared my sandwiches with Bear. I'm sure Sarah didn't have that in mind when she made them for me.

By the time supper came around, we were hungry again.

It was too late to head back. But there was enough time for me to take Thunder and Bear rabbit hunting. I could bring them back and roast them over the fireplace. My father made the best rabbit stew. Unfortunately, I never picked up his cooking talent. I supposed he developed it after mom died.

It went better than I had thought. Thunder wasn't used to a gun going off in his ear. He came close to panicking a few times. But I managed to keep him calm.

The trail wasn't too rough. So, it was a somewhat smooth wagon ride. I have no fucking idea why I hitched him back up to this wagon. Bear enjoyed the free ride.

I did manage to get four rabbits. I'll cook them all tonight. Bear and I'll eat two. One and a half of those will go to Bear. I swear he's is more pig than dog. If I keep a low flame, the other two will hold until morning.

Fuck. Bear's growling again. Shit, Indians. I don't recognize the tribe as one dad and I traded with. These look new and evil. Crap, the way home is blocked. I'm going to back off and hopefully I won't have to make a run of it.

> Jayne slowly mounts Thunder and backs away slowly. She's careful not to spoke Thunder nor the Indians as she turns Thunder around to head off in the opposite direction.
>
> She slowly brings Thunder to a slow trot. She looks back to see Bear following at a distance. So far, it's enough to keep the Indians at bay.
>
> "Oh, fuck me." Jayne has an adrenaline rush as a war cry breaks the air. "Ha!" She brings Thunder up to a full run. Her father taught her that in a situation like this, run. Don't try

to fight your way out. Looking back to shoot takes too much time and you can't see what's in front of you.

Jayne lets out a long loud whistle, "Bear!" Bear comes running at her side. She can feel the wind as arrows nearly miss her head. She's grateful they don't seem to have guns. Or the very least they don't want to waste the bullets on her. Right now, for the very reason she left Daisy at Jake's, she wishes she had her here.

Thunder had speed and endurance. She just didn't know how long he could keep up this pace. Sooner or later, she would be forced to make a stand or surrender. For now, she had to concentrate on keeping the wagon from rolling.

Jaynes heart dropped as she noticed another rider coming at her head on. Jayne drew her pistol. If she has to make a fight of it, she'd rather fight what's in front of her.

As the rider draws near, the figure is that of a woman. She is yelling something at Jayne. She's shooting, but not at Jayne.

"Keep going until you get to the wagons and turn in! I'm right behind you!" The woman ordered as she passed Jayne.

Jayne rode a few yards and saw wooden wagons in a circle. Even the canopies were made of wood. She could hear the woman behind her ordering the wagons to open up.

As soon as Jayne rode in she jumped off her wagon and grabbed her long riffle. She wasted no time in joining the defensive line. The circle closed as the female rider entered.

The Indians stopped before entering gun shot range and made a full retreat. Everyone held their position in the circle, until they were sure the Indians were not coming back.

After about fifteen minutes or so, Jayne heard a silky-smooth female voice come from behind her. "Hey beautiful. I'm glad to see you made it in one piece."

Jayne looked to her left and then to her right. No one was next to her. She turned around to face the voice. With a puzzled look on her face she pointed to herself and asked, "Are you talking to me?"

"I don't see anyone else around." She extends her hand. "They call me Rose."

Jayne shakes the woman's hand. She could feel her body tremble and her heart race. She was an older lady, in her early thirties. She was extremely beautiful and fit. With a shaky voice she replied, "I'm Jayne."

Jayne had never had this reaction to a woman before. She held Rose's hand a little longer than she should have. She quickly let go when she realized her palms were sweaty. She looked away.

Rose gently guided Jayne's head up to face her. "How cute. You're blushing."

Jayne wanted to respond no she wasn't. But she just stood there trembling.

Rose smiled. "There's nothing to be ashamed of." She started walking. "Come with me. We'll secure your wagon and horse for the night. You'll never make it back on your own."

Jayne took Thunder by the reins and followed Rose. Rose stopped in front of the chow wagon. Rose pointed to an empty space. "You can leave your wagon here. Your possessions will be safe with Charlie."

"It's empty." Jayne responded. "I unloaded everything at the ranch."

Rose started speaking to someone else. "Hey Charlie. This is Jayne. She's going to be with us for a while."

Jayne turned. "Hello. I think I'll be here just for the night." Jayne was taken off guard when she realized Charlie was a girl, about her age. Only Charlie breast seemed to bulge out from the top of her blouse.

Charlie walked slowly around Jayne, looking her over. "She's sort of a scrawny thing. I suppose she won't eat much."

Rose reprimanded Charlie. "Behave yourself."

Jayne reached into the back of her wagon and pulled out her rabbits. "I have four rabbits, if that will help?"

Charlie took the rabbits and gave them a look over. "They are as scrawny as she is. I guess I can make it work."

Rose gave Charlie a stern look. "Don't let me have to tell you again."

Charlie walked away.

Rose apologized. "Sorry about Charlie. She's still trying to find her place. Unhitch your horse and we'll bed him down with the others.

Jayne unhitched thunder and followed Rose. Bear finally graced her with his presence.

Rose paused and started petting Bear. "You visited Germany?"

Jayne responded. "I don't even know where that is."

"This is a fine German Shepard you have."

"He was a gift. His name is Bear."

"It fits. We'll wash up and you can relax in my wagon until chow."

"I'll gladly pay for any feed Thunder or Bear uses."

Rose smiled. "There's no need for that. For as long as you're here, what's ours is yours."

"I have to do something."

"We'll talk more about it after chow." Rose lead Jayne to the wash area.

Jayne had never seen a camp like this one before. "This is fucking incredible. You have little tiny cabins on wheels. Even the canopy is made of wood."

Rose smiles, "Each vardo is designed and decorated by the family that owns it. No two are quite the same." Rose points to a vardo near the center of the camp. "That one's mine."

Jayne looks at it with amazement. "Is that a chimney?"

"I guess you can call it that."

"You have a stove in there? You can cook in there?"

"It's a small wood burner. It's good if you get snowed in."

Chow was more of a community gathering, than Jayne expected. Everyone sort of broke off into small groups. But never too far away from the others. Even the families ate outside of their vardo. Multiple conversations would take place from one group to the next. One group could have three separate conversations with three different people from three different groups. Only the sentries remained silent as they ate and kept a watch over their area.

As everyone started breaking up Rose noticed Jayne was missing. She looked around and found

Jayne by her wagon, pulling out her long riffle.

Rose went over to Jayne. "What are you doing?"

Jayne continued checking her riffle over. "I'm going to volunteer for watch."

"The men take care of that. Besides you're our guess."

"I pull my own weight. I can do anything a man can do." Jayne looks up at Rose. In a softer voice, "You've done so much for me already. I have to give something back."

Rose places her hand under Jaynes chin. "The watch is set for the night. In case we're attacked we will need everyone defending the camp. Stop by my vardo in 15 minutes. We will discuss what you can do."

"Okay but, I don't sew, knit or know anything about babies or birthing. Unless it's a foal or calf. I hate chickens."

Before Jayne could complete her list of what she doesn't do, Rose interrupted. "Just be there." Rose shook her head and walked away.

Jayne considered being late. Instead she waited until exactly 15 minutes before knocking at Rose's door.

Rose's voice comes from behind the door. "It's unlocked beautiful, come in."

Jayne opens the door and hesitates when she notices Charlie seated next to Rose.

Charlie looks over at Jayne and gives her a death glare. "I guess I'll be sleeping in the chuck wagon tonight."

Charlie starts to stand up. Rose reaches out and take her by her arm. "Sit that sexy ass down. I'll tell you where you sleep." She looks over at Jayne. "And you, get your ass in her and close the door behind you. You're letting the heat out."

Jayne enters the vardo and close the door. She notices a wood burning stove in the far corner with a log burning in it for warmth. She didn't understand why the room wasn't filled who smoke. She was too focused on Charlie's presence to worry about anything else.

Rose taps the space next to her opposite of where Charlie was seated. "Come and have a seat."

Rose noticed Charlie tensing up. "Mind your place Charlie."

Charlie replied in a barely audible voice. "Yes. Mistress."

Rose looks over at Charlie. "Excuse me?"

Charlie sits upright and answers in a clear voice. "Yes, Mistress."

Jayne sits next to Rose. "I can't stay. I have to get back home. I'll do what I can for you."

Rose turns and looks at Jayne. "Unfortunately, you're going to be with us for a little while. The raiders have the way you came blocked. It's overrun with young warriors trying to prove their worth to their tribe. We planned to stay at this camp site for a few more months. We're pulling up camp in the morning. It won't be long until they return in force."

Jayne replies. "My people are going to come for me."

Rose replies. "We just need you for a few days at the most. We're short a few families. They'll rejoin us along the way." She sighs. "Tomorrow we'll camp just outside of a ton that has a telegraph. You can wire and let your people know, you are fine. Or, you can stay there and wait for them to come get you, after the raiders move on. I hope you decide to stay with us. We need a good scout and hunter."

Jayne asks. "Where are you headed?"

Rose replies and cuts Charlie off as she was about to make some wild comment. "We're going to gather on the outskirts of Carson City, Nevada. From there we'll decide where to go next. I know a wagon master who passes by these parts. You can book passage with him. You'll be safer in numbers."

Jayne thinks for a while. "If I can get a wire through, then okay. I don't want jack to worry."

Charlie asks. "Is that your pa?"

Jayne replies. "No. My pa and ma are dead. Jack is my uncle from my ma side. He and my pa go back as kids."

Charlie seemed to have lost interest. Before Jayne completed her response, Charlie was sorting through one of the storage bins in the vardo. She tossed a large cotton stuffed bedding. She threw out some blankets and three pillows.

Jayne stood up, the best she could. "I'll get going so you can get to bed."

Charlie looks over at Rose. With a puzzled look on her face she lets out a dep sigh. She stops what she's doing and shrugs her shoulders.

Rose responded. "Charlie?" She motions for Charlie to continue setting the bed. Charlie returns to her task without another thought.

Rose replies to Jayne. "You need to be part of a house when you travel with us. There are no loners. You'll eat with Charlie and me. You'll work with us and you will sleep with us. If you have to go out, unless It's a patrol, you'll go with either Charlie, me or we all go as a group. We work as a family and I'm the head of our family. Is that clear?"

Not that Jayne had much of a choice, "Yeah, I guess." Jayne sheepishly replied. Jayne returns to her seat.

Rose replies. "There are some house rules. We'll go over those later." She turned to leave. "I'll be back. I have an elder's meeting to attend."

Charlie adds to the conversation as she continued her task. "No shoes in the vardo, no guns in bed and we clean our messes."

Jayne asks sarcastically, "Anything else?"

Charlie replied in a digging tone. "Yes. We bath."

Jayne's face turned fire red and her fist balled up. "I bath."

"Uh huh.", Charlie was unfazed by Jaynes reaction. She quickly removed Jaynes boots. "Boots go in the corner over there with the other shoes. We'll stop by Mira's vardo after breakfast and have her fitted for house slippers." She untied the holster straps from Jayne's right thigh.

Jayne grabs Charlie's hand. "What are you doing?"

Charlie gives Jayne's hand a quick, sharp smack. Jayne releases her grip. Charlie replies. "No guns in bed." She reaches up and removes Jayne's holster with no further resistance. She opened a cabinet and placed Jayne's holster inside. She points to an empty riffle rack. "Your riffle will go there."

Jayne looked up and saw two riffles already hanging on racks, just below where the roof and wall meets.

Charlie laid back on the bedding and removed all of her clothing. She was as naked as the day she was born. She folded her clothing neatly and placed them in a storage bin under the seats. She looked over at Jayne. "We don't sleep in our clothes.

Jayne was at a lost for words. She's seen a naked woman before. She just wasn't expecting to have this reaction. She actually got wet and her breathing became shallow.

Charlie let out a sigh. Without warning Charlie started undressing Jayne, without resistance. Soon Jayne found herself completely nude alone with another nude woman.

Charlie riffle through some clothing. She tosses a night gown to Jayne. "Try this one on."

Jayne quickly put it on. It went just below her knees. Somehow, she still felt exposed. She could feel her juices beginning to coat her inner walls and outer pussy lips.

Charlie looks Jayne over. "It'll do for now." Charlie slipped on her night gown. It came down just before her ankles.

I don't know why I'm so wet. I don't even like this bitch. She's cute, but she's a bitch. What the fuck. Oh shit, damn. She can kiss.

Charlie had Jayne by the hair, in a full lip lock. She worked her tongue deep inside Jayne's mouth. She forced Jayne's legs apart and slide two fingers deep inside of Jayne's warm and now dripping pussy.

"What the fuck? Oh shit." Jayne sighed.

Charlie's fingers are rubbing right against her spot. Her thumb is locked onto the top of Jayne's clit. She could feel Jayne weakening at her knees.

Charlie tightens her grip and increases the speed. She pulls Jayne's head all the way back by her hair. She whispers in Jayne's ear. "You're mine tonight bitch." She starts kissing slowly down Jayne's neck.

As much as Jayne wanted to take control. She knew she was right. She was her puppet, her bitch. At least for the night.

Charlie released her grip on Jayne just long enough to slip her nightgown up and off from over her head. She resumed her grip between Jaynes leg even tighter and more forceful. Her fingers slammed against Jayne's spot without mercy.

Jayne could hear the sloshing of her juices, as Charlie allowed her to fall slowly to her knees. She forced Jayne onto her back by pulling her hair. She kept Jayne's hips raised up off the bedding.

Jayne was dripping wet and on the edge of exploding, when she heard the door open. Jayne struggled to break free. Charlie's grip on her cunt was unbreakable. The more she struggled the more she wanted to cum. It was the only thing Jayne had left. She struggled through each orgasmic wave to deny Charlie her victory.

Suddenly Charlie released her grip and pulled out making sure to drag her unyielding fingers over her spot, as quickly and forcefully as she could. Charlie's hand and fingers were covered with Jayne's juices. All Jayne could do was quiver, as she denied herself full release.

Rose closed the door and stated to Charlie. "You wasted no time. Impressive."

Charlie proudly answered. "Thank you, Mistress. I was just getting her broken in for you. She's a wild one." Charlie raised up her hand as Jayne's juices ran down her arm, to display her bounty. "Want a taste."

Rose took hold of Charlie's arm and sucked Jayne's juices from her fingers.

Jayne watched as Charlie ritually and slowly removed her Mistress' clothing. Folding each item with care and stored them away. Charlie bowed down with her arms extended towards her Mistress, palms up.

Rose walked over to Jayne and knelt between her still quivering legs. She lifted Jayne's legs over her shoulder, to better inspect Charlie's work.

Rose lowered Jayne down until she was flat on her back. She reached up with both hands and took hold of Jayne's nipples as firmly as she could. She twisted and pulled them. Jayne felt a jolt of electricity and excitement mixed with an unbelievable amount of pain. She wanted it to never end.

Rose looked up from between Jayne's legs. "You don't cum until I give you permission. Is that clear?"

Jayne could only nob yes. If she taken the breathes needed to speak, she would have exploded on the spot.

Rose asked Charlie, "Why are you over there? I want her to taste your pussy as I taste her. I want you to cum in her mouth, as she cum in mine."

Charlie responded. "Yes, Mistress." She walked over to Jayne's head, taking care not to step on her Mistress. She took hold of Jayne's shoulder. "On three?"

Rose gripped Jayne's hips and rapidly counted down. "One, two, three."

Jayne quickly found herself on her side. Her back firmly against the storage walls. Rose inverted her position and locked Jayne's legs securely in place, under her arms. Rose's tongue flapped vigorously against the tip of Jayne's clitoris.

Charlie whispered in Jayne's ear. "You're going to eat my pussy, lap up every drop, my little bitch." She removed her nightgown and straddled Jayne's face and planted her face between her Mistress' thighs.

Jayne obeyed without question. Charlie's pubic area and legs were silky smooth. Her pussy was shaven completely clean. Jayne had never imagined that before.

Jayne did her best to mimic how Rose was devouring her. She noticed that Charlie would tighten her pussy walls as she fought off orgasm after orgasm.

Without warning Rose spread Jayne's ass cheeks as far apart as possible. The rush of cool air raced across Jayne's exposed asshole. Jayne could now longer hold back. She exploded in one continuous orgasmic wave.

It was like a chain reaction. Charlie exploded and released her juices into Jayne's mouth. Jayne lapped up every drop as instructed. Rose in turn orgasm. Charlie cleaned her Mistress inner chambers, leaving not a drop behind.

After they laid still for a while, Rose tossed the pillows up towards the top of the bed. She unfolded a blanket.

Charlie leaned in to kiss Jayne goodnight. Jayne pulled away. Charlie pulled her back and gave her a firm, long and wet lip lock. Their lips and faces were still dripping from pussy juices.

When Charlie finally released her grip. They slowly parted as drizzles of juices clung like a bridge between their parting lips.

Rose broke the silence. "This is one of our most important house rules. We never go to bed with grievances. We always kiss one another goodnight. When we're leaving or returning, we give each other a kiss. We're a family under this vardo. We stand together as one, be it in here or out there. Right or wrong, we're a family." She leans in and kisses each of them goodnight and pulls the blanket over all three of them.

Jaye asks, "What if our family member is wrong?"

"Out there be it in camp out outside of camp. We stand as one. Our tribe is one. Our family is one. Right or wrong, we stick together." Rose touches Jayne's leg under the blanket. Rose continues. "I handle all disciplinary issues for this family. I have the final word and issue punishment as I feel fit."

Without another word all three ladies feel fast asleep. Jayne had never slept so content in her life. Suddenly she was awakened by a sharp slap across her bare bottom.

She instinctively went for the gun under her pillow. She couldn't find her gun. She turned to fight and saw it Charlie kneeling next to her.

"What the fuck, Charlie?" the startled Jayne exclaimed.

"Time to move that ass sweet cheeks," Charlie replied with a smile.

The rooster crowed. Jayne sighed and asked, "Where are my clothes?" She grabbed for a blanket to cover herself. The blankets had been removed.

Charlie points to the side of the vardo. "Lift that cushion. Your clothes are over there. Your gun is in the cabinet just to your right. Your riffle is on the rack."

"Do you mind?" Jayne asked.

Charlie chuckled. "After last night, you choose now to be modest?" She regains her composure. "I drew you a bath, out back. There is a curtain you can pull across for privacy." She points to the far former by the door. "Soap and towels are over there. Mira dropped off two pair of slippers. One is for when you are in the vardo and the other is for outside. Like when you go out to bath." Charlie couldn't resist, "I guess your feet aren't as big as they look. I thought for sure it was a custom job."

Jayne became defensive. "My feet are a normal size, I bathe. I don't smell."

Charlie had to fight to hold off a full belly laugh. "I was just messing with you. You may want to bathe though. You're still wearing me across your face."

Without saying another word. An embarrassed Jayne wrapped herself in a towel, put on a pair of slippers and headed off for a bathe.

Chapter 5

The Long Way Home

Not that I didn't enjoy our little fuck feast. I have to get back and let Jake know I'm alright. Looks like these Indians set up camp along the main road. There's another path I can take. I can't take the wagon, but I take thunder. He's no Daisy, but if I have to make a run of it, he's no slouch. This way is a bit rocky. If I keep going, I should make Jake's just a little after nightfall.

Crap. It looks like an entire tribe. Hopefully they're passing through. Pa told me stories of tribes migrating to either follow the buffalo or traveling to a warmed climate to wait out the winter. Usually you can trade with them. But there were tribes, who wiped out entire settlements. If this is a hostile tribe, my best chance is to alert the military. I'm going to kick some ass if they took my father's hat.

Shit, now I have to go back to the gypsy camp and travel with them to the next town. I can let Jake know I'm alright and warn him about the tribe moving through. I swear, if that bitch calls me sweet checks in public one more time, I'm going to knock her on her ass.

At least I'll make lunch. Gypsy stew, yummy. It's better than starvation, I guess. After lunch I'm assigned to the hunting party. I guess I should head back before I get my ass caught.

When Jayne arrived back at camp, it was quieter than she expected. Everyone was broken off into family units and eating next to their vardo. She put away and tended to Thunder, before making her way back to Rose's vardo.

Jayne met Rose as she was exiting the door. Jayne asked, "I thought everyone ate meals as a group."

"Only dinner and special feasts. All other meals are times for family. Charlie went to get our portion. She'll return soon."

A few minutes later, Charlie returned. She was followed by a young man, carrying a small caldron filled with hot stew. Charlie pointed to the rigging over an open flame near the vardo. She smiled and asked in a soft voice, "Could you be so kind and set it up there?"

"Yes, sure." Replied the young man as he struggled.

After he setup the caldron and left Jayne remarked in a condescending tone, "A slave of yours'?"

"Don't worry your pretty little head sweet checks." Charlie replied. "You're still my number one."

Jayne's face turned pale.

Before Jayne could respond, Rose interrupted. "Enough! Take your seats. It's family time.

Jayne reluctantly complied.

Charlie kissed Jayne on her cheek and whispered. "Don't you worry. No one can replace you sweet cheeks."

Jayne was bursting with anger. It was all she could do, not to completely loose her temper. She barely touched her meal.

After lunch. Jayne started towards the vardo. Charlie asked, "Where are you going?"

"I'm going to get my riffle. I'm on the hunting detail."

Rose interjected. "The hunt is postponed until the threat of attack is over. We can't spare the bullets."

Jayne asked. "What do you need for me to do?"

Rose replied. "We're moving out after dinner. The Indians will not attack at after nightfall. I'll drive the Vardo. Charlie you will drive Rose's wagon. We put extra barrels of water in it. And you Jayne will ride scot. I need the two of you well rested. We'll be traveling most of the night." She pointed towards the Vardo. "The two of you need to go inside and take a nap."

Charlie started towards the Vardo. "Yes, Mistress."

Jayne responded sharply. "A nap? I haven't taken a nap since I was twelve."

Rose placed her hand under Jayne's chin and tilted her head up. "Don't you ever speak to me in that tone again. You will walk in there and so as you are told. The only choice you have is rather you're going to do it before I bae your ass and beat it red, or after."

After Rose released her grip, Jayne stood her ground for a few seconds. She then turned and headed inside.

Rose sternly asked, "Excuse me?"

Taken off guard by Rose's tone and threat, Jayne sheepishly replied under her breathe, "Yes, Mistress."

"Were you speaking to me? I couldn't hear you." Rose snapped.

Jayne stopped, cleared her throat and turned towards Rose. "Yes, Mistress." She responded in a loud clear voice. She fought to hold back tears.

"Better." Replied Rose. "Don't worry, soon you will have an enough reason to cry." Rose turned and walked away.

The slackened Jayne entered the Vardo and removed her boots. She was startled when the nightshirt Charlie tossed to her landed on her head. "What the fuck Charlie?" Jayne barked as she trough the nightshirt to the ground.

Charlie responded with a smile. "First, there is no cussing inside. Secondly, we don't sleep in our clothes."

Jayne picks up the nightshirt and hung it on the door knob. She started undressing. "I'm not a baby, who needs to be sent off to nap."

"We're not the only ones taking a nap." Charlie replied. "Everyone who is working tonight are sleeping. You have to be at your best."

As they get into the bed, Charlie laid out, Jayne added. "I'm not your slave."

"Charlie explained. "of that you're right. We're both the slaves of Mistress Rose. Since I'm her number one, that puts you beneath me. So, by order of rank, you are my slave."

Jayne snapped. "Rose isn't my Mistress."

"She became your Mistress the second you called her Mistress. You could have answered yes Madame. But, you answered, Yes, Mistress." Charlie smirked. "At that moment, you became my bitch. You can easily kick my ass, yet you yield your will to me."

"I yield nothing. I'm no one's bitch."

Charlie threw back the covers, raise her nightshirt up over her hips. She spread her legs and exposed her clean-shaven pussy. She grabbed Jayne by the back od her hair. "Yes, you are. And I'll prove it." She pulled Jayne's face between her thighs, inches from her now wet pussy. "You're going to eat my pussy. I'm going to cum in your mouth and you're going to lick me clean."

Before Jayne could respond, Charlie pulled her face deep against her pussy. Jayne struggled at first, but soon gave in. She was shocked that she was wet. She was excited by the force Charlie applied. Every time Jayne pulled back Charlie forced her face deeper. At times she almost pasted out from lack of air.

When she slowed down Charlie tightened her grip on her hair. She lifted her head up and gave her a rapid series of sharp slaps across her face. "Bitch! I didn't say stop." Charlie barked and forced Jayne's face back in place.

Jayne doesn't know when it began. She had come to crave the pain. The closer Charlie came to orgasm, the more eagerly Jayne licked and sucked her juices. When Charlie came to orgasm, Charlie locked Jaynes head in place, until Jayne lapped her dripping pussy clean.

As sharply as it began, it ended. When Charlie was satisfied, she pushed Jayne away. "You did good, sweet cheeks." She pulled the covers over them.

An extremely horny and wet Jayne asked, "What about me?"

"What about you bitch?" Charlie calmly replied. "You receive pleasure only when Mistress or I decide you deserve it. If I catch you touching yourself, I'll tie your hands up above your head." She kissed Jayne on her lips. "Now get some sleep sweet cheeks."

Jaye never thought it possible. She fell asleep in Charlie's arms. Although she was horny as hell, she felt secure. She never felt this way about another woman. It scared and excited her.

Charlie was awakened by Charlie cleaning her face with a wet towel. "Hey beautiful. We can't sleep forever. Super is on in 15 minutes."

Jayne smiled. She didn't say anything. She helped Charlie fold and put away the bedding. When she went to get her clothes, Charlie stopped her. Mistress wants to speak with you first."

"Why can't I be dressed when she talks with me?"

"Just wait for her. I'll be back afterwards,"

Before another word could be said Rose entered. "Charlie, could you excuse your sister and me?" Rose requested in a calm yet stern voice.

"Yes, Mistress." Charlie replied. She looked into the eyes of a terrified Jayne as she left.

Rose sat down and ordered, "Come here."

A terrified Jayne complied. Before she could say a word, Rose pulled her over her lap and yanked her nightshirt up over her hips with such force it lifted Jayne up off her lap for a moment and the nightshirt almost rose up over her head.

Rose forced Jayne down so her head was inches from the floor and her ass was up and fully exposed. Rose wasted no time. The first smack was sharp and firm. It caused Jayne's ass to quiver. It was quickly followed by a stead rhythm.

A shocked Jayne struggled, but couldn't break free. She couldn't even get a hand back to protect her now burning ass. As much as she fought back the tears she soon burst out in a full sob. She was crying uncontrollably like a baby.

Just when Jayne thought it was over, it got worst. Rose started on her virgin legs with the back of a wooden hair brush. She slowly and methodically worked her way back to Jaynes throbbing ass.

Jayne became worked up into a frenzy. She tried to kick, but Rose held her legs as securely in place as she held the rest of her body. Her ass and legs were at her Mistress mercy.

What confused Jayne the most was the second the hair brush struck her already throbbing and tender ass, she had a full orgasm. She was embarrassed and overcome with a pleasure never felt before. How can pain become pleasurable and craved. Her sobbing became more intense.

Rose stopped as quickly as she began. She released her grip on Jayne. Jayne immediately grabbed and rubbed her throbbing ass and upper legs. She slowly sank between her Mistress' legs, still sobbing loudly and uncontrollably.

Rose gently lifted her up until she was seated on her lap. She tilted Jayne's head up and kissed her gently, yet deeply on her lips. "I love you and would die for you. This is your home for as long as you want or need it to be. You're always welcomed here. But you will never speak to me like that again. Are we clear little one?"

"Yes, Mistress." The tearful Jayne replied.

"Supper is in three minutes. Pull yourself together and get dressed. I expect you not to be any more than five minutes late."

"Yes, Mistress."

Rose left. As promised, Charlie entered before the door closed. "That wolf of yours is strong and loyal to you. There were times I almost lost control of him. He wanted to claw threw the door."

Charlie pulled the nightshirt, which was up around Jayne's head, off. "Bend over the bench." Charlie continued.

Jaynes's face went pale and her heart sank.

Charlie comforted her fears. "I'm not going to spank you. I have something to help with the pain."

Jayne slowly bent over the bench. Her quivering and throbbing ass was once again exposed and at the mercy of another. She clinched at Charlies first touch. She quickly relaxed when she felt the cool soothing elixir being gently applied to her ass and upper legs.

"Relax, little one." Charlie's voice was reassuring. "This is a message oil we use." Jayne orgasmed unexpectedly when Charlie rubbed the oil between her legs, slipping her finger deep inside Jaynes dripping and quivering pussy.

Charlie stood Jayne upright. Jayne didn't move as Charlie went and got her clothes. Charlie started dressing Jayne as she stood in total submission.

Once Jayne was dressed, Charlie wiped the tears from her face with a damp cloth. Afterwards Charlie wiped the oil from her hand. "We need to get to supper sweet cheeks."

Jayne followed, with her head lowered.

On the way Charlie added. "Mistress didn't do this to break your will. What we do as a family, stays with our family. Out here, I need you to be fearless. I need for you to be the Jayne you were when I first met you. The Jayne I fell in love with."

Jayne smiled and lifted her head. "I can still kick your ass."

I know, A smirking Charlie replied. "Perhaps one day you will. I need you fully alert tonight."

Before Charlie could respond, Rose announced in a loud and joyful voice. "There my two girls are. Another minute and we would have started supper without you."

Jayne sat next to Rose. She felt safe and protected next to her. Despite the intense spanking her ass was still throbbing from. Jayne had the need to be as close to Rose as possible. From time to time she rested her head on Rose's shoulder.

Charlie was seated next to Rose, opposite of Jayne. She sat as close to Rose as possible as well.

After dinner and everything was secure, they struck camp and headed out. It was strange for Rose to have someone else drive her wagon. The fact that it was Charlie was a little better. But, not by much.

For the most part. Bear stayed at Jaynes side. When she returned to report her findings to the wagon master Vikas, the Elder, Bear would hitch a ride on the wagon, under Charlie's legs. When it was Jaynes rotation to go out scouting, Bear was at her side without fail.

Jayne's ass and thighs felt every time the saddle slapped against her ass. Jayne concealed her secret pain. It gave her sort of a strange pride.

Their evening trek went without event. They came to a clearing and circled the wagons. Jayne and the others who worked throughout the night were relieved by sentries.

Jayne tied Thunder to a tree next to the Vardo. Charlie met up with her.

"Come sweet cheeks. Let's get some sleep. The stable hands with tend to, fed and water Thunder." Charlie took Jayne by the hand and led her inside.

Once inside, they dressed for bed, which had been laid out ahead of time by Rose. Rose was already in bed. They got into bed on either side of Rose. Jayne fell fast asleep as soon as her head hit the pillow.

Chapter 6

The slow journey

It's been four fucking days and my ass is still sore. I tried using my duster as a cushion. That didn't work. I made things worse. I don't know why I even let them touch me. There's something about Rose. I can't put my hand on it. But I'm drawn to her, like she's some fucking flame and I'm a moth.

She holds herself with a certain pride. Even living out here with no real place to call home. When I look into her eyes, or hear her voice, I go weak. I lose my will to resist her. She has never once asked me to do so, but when I call her Mistress something, I can't explain washes over me. It's like I found my place. I'm not going to become a fucking gypsy.

I have nothing against gypsies, my father traded with them all of the time. Papa use to always say, 'if you threat a person with respect, they will treat you with respect as well.'

Charlie is a pain in the ass. I don't know how we became a thing. I don't even like women. Of all of the times I've had sex, I've only been fucked by a man twice. There's something wrong with that.

The thing is, she doesn't even ask anymore. Yesterday, we came upon a lake, I figured I'd have a bath and swim. There was just us girls. I'm sure there were guys somewhere sneaking a peak. When I got out, I looked for my towel. It was not where I put it.

Charlie had it. She ran into the woods. I wouldn't had bothered, but she had my clothes as well. I had no choice but to follow her. She stopped. When I went to get the towel, she attacked me. Not like she was robbing me or anything.

She grabbed me by the back of my hair and pulled my head back. She reached between my legs and forced them apart. It was so quick I lost my balance. Charlie held me up and in place by my hair and she shoved her two middle fingers deep inside me. She spread them as far apart as she could. I thought she was going to rip me apart.

It was the roughest finger bang I ever had. Her thumb was pressed firmly against the top of my clit. She brought me to the edge of orgasm at least three times. Each time she forbidden me from orgasm.

I've never felt so alive in my life. It was both terrifying and exhilarating at the same time. For the first time she scared me. At the same time, I trusted her more than anyone I have ever trusted in my life.

When she finally did allow me to cum, I was a mess. My entire body convulsed. I covered my mouth so not to be heard. As I fell to the ground, she held onto me by my cunt.

She didn't let go even when I hit the ground. She knelt down and supported me by placing her knee in the small of my back. She wrapped her free arm around my waist and held me firmly in place. She spread her fingers apart until I was opened up as much as possible.

I was breathless. I struggled for every breath. She thrusted her fingers so deep inside me I could feel her knuckles with each thrust. She moved her hand side to side, up and down and in every and any direction she pleased.

I was beyond orgasm. I was wow! It was like I was in another reality. A place I can't describe. A feeling so pleasurable it was beyond words. I heard her voice in a distance. As if she was calling me back. I never wanted to leave.

When I did come to my senses, I realized something I hadn't before. Charlie no longer had possession of me. My head never hit the ground. I fell into Charlie's lap. It was Rose who did this to me.

Rose removed her hand from me and Charlie after gently laying down my head, sucked and licked her Mistress' fingers and hand clean.

When her slave completed her task. Rose lowered my hips to the ground. I was convulsing and quivering uncontrollably. She held me down and kissed me firmly on the mouth. I welcomed her kiss. I moved my head forward several times as she pulled away. She responded by kissing me even deeper. When she stopped, she looked me in the eye.

She said, 'You've done well little one. I'm so proud of you and I love you very much.'

My response took me by surprise. 'I love you too. Thank you, Mistress.'

I don't know how I got there. I woke up in the vardo, in my nightshirt and under the covers. I would have thought it was a dream, but my pussy was so sore. It was as if someone drove a wagon train through me. But I wasn't bleeding, and I wasn't torn. I checked. I don't remember when Rose arrived and took over. Maybe she was there all the while. Maybe Charlie only lured me in, and Rose took me from behind. I never saw the face of the person who had me by my cunt. I only assumed it was Charlie. What if it was Mistress, um I mean Rose all of the time.

Jayne stops her horse and looks around. "Bear! I spill my heart to you and there you are licking yourself. Men, I give up. You're all alike. Two legs or four, pigs." She signals for Bear to follow, "Come on. We only have a few hours left. It's almost sunrise."

"Oh, you know what Bear?" Jayne looked at the uninterested dog. "A couple days back when we were in Lucin. I sent a telegram to Jake. So, he wouldn't worry. They charged me $2.50 to have the telegram delivered to Jake's house. That was on top of the $1.25 to send it. I had to send it. It could sit for days at the telegraph office, before Jake rode into town. I asked him to telegraph me at Cabra, Nevada, our next stop."

Jayne sighed as she scanned her surroundings. "Gypsies move so slow. It's not as if we're running from a band of murderous Indians or anything."

Chapter 7

Dark nights

Finally, after five fucking days we're making camp about a mile outside of Cabra, Nevada. We're going to be here for a while. Maybe a few days or so. It will give me time to relax and get into town and check on Jake's telegraph.

I rode into town. I figured we could do some shopping. At first, they were hesitant, nut I soon convinced them. We took my wagon and Bear tagged along. A few of the guys would meet up with us later. They needed to pick up some supplies for the camp. They were going to load it onto the wagon.

When we got into town, I went right for the general store to check for a telegraph. Jake sent it a d=few days ago. He said he was glad to hear from me. When Ricky and Clayton arrived at my ranch it was over run by Indians. Clayton rode back and gathered some men to fight them off. They searched for me afterwards, but there were just too many of them. He said it looks as if the tribe is just moving through. A group of young bucks were trying to prove themselves as warriors. Since my caravan is going to Carson City, he wants me to wait for Ricky and Clayton there. He also wired $100.00 to me from my account.

It felt as if the entire town was watching us. We went nowhere alone. The merchant at the general store watched us like a hawk. I dropped off the order for supplies. It will take a couple days for him to complete the order. He tried to get full payment up front. I told him 50% now and 50% when he delivers, else we'll take out business to the next town. He agreed.

There wasn't much to do in Cabra. We still had to wait for the guys before we headed back. There was a saloon in town. I saw people ordering lunch. We decided to go there. It wasn't anything fancy. A saloon is a saloon, I guess.

> The saloon was almost full. Jayne took a moment to familiarize herself with the environment. She found a table, that was reasonably clean. She signaled for a server.
>
> A server came over and asked, "What can I get for you today?" She seemed a little nervous.
>
> Jayne replied, "Yes, we need to see lunch menus. What's your special for today?"

"Just a minute." The server went over and spoke with the bar tender.

Laci, one of the women with Jayne started to get up. "We should just leave."

Jayne motioned for her to take her seat. "Sit down. We're just here to eat lunch like everyone else."

The bartender slowly made his way to their table. "I'm sorry ladies. The kitchen is closed."

Jayne started pointing out customers. "How is your kitchen closed? You just took an order from them and they were just served food from the kitchen."

The bartender leaned in. "What I meant to say is that the kitchen is closed to your kind."

Jayne became upset. "What the fuck do you mean by my kind? The kind with money?"

The bartender interrupted. "I don't care who you stole it from. But you have to leave."

Before Jayne could respond, Charlie took her hand. "It's not worth it. We'll return to camp." She and the other women stood up to leave. Charlie looked down at Jayne. "Let's go little one."

Jayne stood up. As they exited Jayne tipped over the table. As they reached the door a loud click broke the air and the room fell silent. Without looking Jayne turned around in the direction of the shotgun chambering a round, drew her revolver, knelt and fired.

Her round struck the shotgun as it was baring down and knocked the barrel up and a round discharged. It took the bartender by surprise and he lost his grip. The shotgun flew across the bar.

Jayne responded, "We may not be fit to eat your food. You pull a gun on us again; I will see to it that what's left of you isn't fit for the undertaker." She backed out of the saloon after her friends left. And started walking back towards their wagon.

A shaken Laci asked, "Will you really shot him?"

"If I have to." Jayne responded. "Out here, you shot first or you die."

Charlie replies. "We try to avoid that."

"What did he mean by your kind?" asked Jayne.

"Gypsies", Charlie answered. "When people think of gypsies, they think of thieves and con-artists. We are neither. Although, there are some who follow that path."

A confused Jayne looked at Charlie. "I've met gypsies before. I've never seen a vardo, until now. You live like gypsies, but you don't sound or look like one."

Charlie was eager to answer. "People thing gypsies are from Romania. So, a lot of Romanians pass as gypsies. I guess, if you live a certain way long enough it becomes who you are. So, from that perspective you can call them gypsies."

Charlie took a breath and leaned against a hitching post. "Gypsies, are from India."

Jayne interrupted. "You don't look Indian. What tribe are you from?"

Charlie sighed. She couldn't help but smile. "I said I'm from India. India is a country across the oceans. I'm technically an Indian, because I'm from India. But I'm not one of the natives, from here."

Jayne replied. "I knew you weren't American, because of the way you speak, and your skin is so smooth and silky, like a caramel apple you get from the fair, but darker."

One of Charlie's favorite pastime has become, making Jayne blush. She leaned in and whispered in Jayne's ear. "You like it darker, don't you? I know you dream about my dark silky pussy in your face."

Jayne turned bright red and then flush. She stumbled her way onto the wagon and took up the reins.

Charlie slid in besides her and took the reins. In a low voice she said. "I'll take us back sweet cheeks."

Charlie took her time on the road back. Jayne didn't notice. She was too lost in thought, over what happened with Charlie.

When Jayne started paying attention, she realized they were no longer on the trail back to camp. They were in a heavily wooded area. Jayne asked, "Where are we?"

Charlie stopped the wagon. "We need to ask you something."

Jayne looked around for the other two girls. She saw they were in the wagon, just behind her seat. Laci, and Maliyah poised in anticipation of her answer. "What? Asked Jayne.

"You do understand the relationship between Mistress and me?" Charlie asked.

"I know you have some sort of relationship. I don't judge. It's none of my business.", Jayne replied. "I just don't understand why you call her Mistress."

For the first time Charlie became nervous and started breathing shallow. "She's my Mistress, because I'm her submissive. What that mean, is that I've freely agreed to submit every aspect of my life to her, her rules, her sexual desires and her punishments."

"So, you're like a slave?"

"Yes and no. I prefer submissive. I'm free to leave anytime I want."

"What does that have to do with me?"

Charlie slid her hand up Jayne's inner thigh to her crotch and started gently messaging her. "I was just curious. You never resisted anything I did to you. You can kick my ass ten times over. Yet here I sit, with my hand in your pants, with two fingers in your pussy. You haven't resisted me yet. Are you a submissive? Do you dream of being totally dominated?"

"Jayne shakenly replied. "I'm submissive to no man."

Charlie leaned in, "I'm not a man. I'm collared by Mistress Rose. Laci and Maliyah are collared by Master Soneji."

"What do you mean collared?" Jayne asked.

Charlie explained. "When a submissive pledge herself to her Mistress."

Laci and Maliyah interrupts in concert. "Or, Master!"

"Or Master." Charlie added. "There is a collaring ceremony where the submissive receives their Mistress' or Master's collar."

They point to choker styled necklaces around their necks.

Jayne examined them. "I seen them. I thought they were some sort of Gypsy jewelry."

Charlie removed Jayne's holster, without resistance. She pushed Jayne back and pulled off her boots and then pants and panties.

Jayne attempted to cover herself. Laci and Maliyah held her hands over her head, as Charlie spread her legs apart.

"It's clear she's one of us." Maliyah stated. "We just have to figure where she fits in on the pecking order."

Jayne was embarrassed. She was so wet. "Let's say I am a submissive. But only with women. I don't know anyone other than Rose and she's your Mistress."

Charlie explained. "A Mistress or Master may take as many submissive or slaves as they can care for. A submissive or slave can only have one Mistress or Master. Mistress would be more than pleased to claim you."

"I have a ranch. I have a life." Jayne replied.

Charlie responded. "You don't have to be collared, to continue being part of our family. You can work out with Mistress your agreement and still run your ranch."

"How would that work?"

"That is between Mistress and yourself." Charlie answered. "We organize ourselves into small groups. When we go out, we can watch over each other." Charlie gently caressed between Jayne's thighs, sliding her fingers in and out of her. "You're my cunt, sweet cheeks. We just want to know where you fit in with our little group."

Jayne was confused yet offered no resistance. "So, you would be my Mistress?"

"That would make us sister subs. I would be like the big sister." Charlie explained.

"So, that would make them out=r cousins?"

"Something like that." Charlie answered. "So, what do you say sweet cheeks?"

Jayne was in a very exposed position. She didn't struggle to free herself. "I will not give myself to a Master. I have nothing against men. I just don't want one over me. There are too many men in my life trying to control me as it is. What would I even say to Rose?"

"You just speak to her and tell her your feelings." Charlie kissed Jayne's stomach. "Then the two of you will work out the details."

"Every detail will not be settled in one day. Your ranch and other property will still be yours. Including your wolf. Just tell her what you want and what you're willing to do or not do."

Laci interrupted, "She's clearly one of us."

Maliyah completed her thought. "It's time we initiated her." She produced a straight razor, a razor strap, a bowl and canteen of water.

"What?" was all Jayne could muster. The implements took her by surprise.

Charlie attached one end of the razor strap to the side of the wagon and began sharpening the razor as Laci and Maliyah held Jayne's legs securely spread apart and her knees to her shoulders.

Charlie soaped up Jaynes public hair. "There are no wholly mammoths in our sisterhood. It's all smooth sailing from her on out." She began shaving Jayne's public regions. "Besides your hair was getting stuck between my teeth."

Although Charlie was careful not to cut Jayne, she was far from gentle. She handled Jayne like a pro. She probed Jayne and moved her into position after position. She pulled her lips out and apart, to chase down any and all stray hairs. She even shaved the peach fuzz that sprouted around her anus.

When Charlie concluded, Jayne was clean shaven. Charlie even applied some very sweet-smelling oil. "Any sister can inspect any other sister at any time, without warning. If found unshaven, that sister is subject to being shaven on the spot and any other punishment the sister who found her desires." Charlie christened her work with a kiss. "Understood?"

"Yes." Jayne was both too excited and embarrassed to say anything further.

Charlie added. "When it's just us together, even if just two of us, we address each other as sister. But I get to call you sweet cheeks."

"Yes, sister." Jayne answered.

Maliyah lifted her dress up over her hips exposing her bare and clean shave pussy. "I'm officially bored. We also have full access to each other, when our Master or Mistress isn't using us." She straddled Jaynes face. "Let's see if you're as legendary with your tongue as you are with that pistol."

Jayne had no choice but to surrender. She slid her tongue in and out of Maliyah's slick silky slit. Charlie buried her face deep inside of Jayne, and Laci lifted Charlie's dress and started a crusade of being her to orgasm.

I don't believe this. I'm not going to become everyone's bitch. It's bad enough, I'm Charlie's bitch. I had no idea I would enjoy being with another woman, let alone three.

Just as Jayne was about to bring Maliyah to orgasm, Maliyah got up. Charlie quickly took her place, as they switched places. Jayne soon learned that Laci took eating pussy extremely seriously.

Fuck me. Wow! What the fuck? Did that slut just spit inside my pussy?

Laci spread Jayne's pussy as far apart as she could and spit right down her open hole. Jayne's entire body quivered.

Oh fuck. She's actually nibbling on my clit. Jayne found herself at the edge of exploding. Laci would back off each time. Jayne's mind was in a tail spin. I definitely can't let this bitch dominate me, Jayne thought as she bared down on Charlie's dripping pussy.

Just as Jayne was about to cum, they switched again. They continued switching on Jayne denying her the pleasure of release. Although each of them orgasm.

As quickly as it began it ended. Leaving Jayne thriving and at the edge of exploding. Laci and Maliyah held her arms up over her head as Charlie held her legs spread apart.

Jayne finally surrendered and the single word she's never uttered to another woman came from her lips. "Please."

"Yes, my love." Charlie answered as she buried her face deep between her and brought her to multiple orgasms.

Jayne thrived and moaned. She had no words. Charlie let her lay there for a while and then helped her get dressed.

It was dark when they returned to camp. Laci and Maliyah took care of the wagon, horse and rigging. Charlie made the bed. Jayne went fast to sleep.

"Rise and shine sweet cheeks."

Jayne awaken to Charlie's face inched from her face. "What the fuck? What time is it?"

"Almost lunch."

"Oh fuck, the supplies!"

"Arie was pissed. I told him we threw a wheel. He went into town early. He and the others are back."

"Why did you let me sleep so long?"

"Mistress told me to. I told her that you were one of us. She knew we initiated you. She figured you needed your rest."

"What do I say to her?"

"Nothing in your nightshirt. Get dressed, have lunch and speak with her after lunch." Charlie hands Jayne a wrinkled-up letter. "Arie picked this up from the general store. It's for you."

Jayne read the letter. "It's a telegram from Jake. Apparently, the Indians are still in the area. He received a telegram from a shipping company. I'm expecting a shipment to arrive in a month. He wants me to wait for him in Carson City."

"What type of shipment?" A curious Charlie enquired.

"I don't know. He didn't say."

"Nothing you can do about it now. I guess we're stuck with you until Carson City."

Lunch was eye opening for Jayne. For the first time she noticed the different dynamics of the families. The entire camp was divided into Mistresses and Masters and submissive and slaves. There were even male submissive and slaves and some even had Masters.

Jayne had never imagined a male submissive, let alone one owned by another man.

About an hour after lunch, Jayne walked sheepishly over to Rose. "Excuse me Mistress." Jayne stated with a shaky voice.

"Yes, little one," Rose responded as she stroked Jayne's hair.

Jayne was unable to speak. She was too nervous to put her thoughts into words.

"I'll make it easy for you. I know why you're here little one." Rose lifted Jayne's head. "I'll train you until we reach Carson City. At that time, it will be up to you if you want to be collared. We can work out the details then. Your ranch and everything you own will always be yours. Ok?"

"Yes, Mistress."

"Good girl. Now strip. I want to take a better look at you."

A hesitant Jayne replied. "Here, in public?"

"If I tell you to strip and walk down the middle of town square, you will do it. Is that clear?"

"Yes, Mistress." Jayne stripped. She stood nude and embarrassed.

"Put your hands behind your head. Elbows all the way back and legs spread as far apart as you can get them. I want you on your toes."

Jayne did as she was instructed.

Rose circled and inspected her new prize. She spread Jayne's legs further apart. "Get dressed. Go find your sister and help her with clean up."

"Yes, Mistress."

Fuck, all I wanted was a few fucking rabbits for supper. Now I have a Mistress, three sister subs and I'm on my way to Carson City. At least I have my father's ranch back. I don't know what she means by training, but I guess I'll find out soon enough.

The End.